FIESTA

by Coach John Wooden

with Steve Jamison
and Bonnie Graves

Illustrated by
Susan F. Cornelison

Perfection Learning®

Editorial Director: Susan C. Thies
Editor: Twyla Anderson
Design Director: Randy Messer
Designer: Tobi S. Cunningham

For information, contact
Perfection Learning® Corporation
1000 North Second Avenue, P.O. Box 500
Logan, Iowa 51546-0500
Phone: 1-800-831-4190
Fax: 1-800-543-2745
perfectionlearning.com

2 3 4 5 6 PP 16 15 14 13 12
PP / 4 / 12

Paperback ISBN-10: 0-7891-7187-2
ISBN-13: 978-0-7891-7187-0

Reinforced Library Binding ISBN-10: 0-7569-7791-6
ISBN-13: 978-0-7569-7791-2

CONTENTS

CHAPTER 1

Looking Like Losers

"What's the matter, Inch and Miles?" Lily asked.

Inch frowned.

Miles slumped in his desk.

"International Day," said Inch.

"It's a dumb idea," said Miles.

"Wrong," said Lily. "It's going to be way fun! Tulip and I are going to do a Russian dance. We're making costumes too," she said.

Lily waved her costume drawings in front of Inch and Miles. "So what are you going to do for International Day?" Lily asked.

Miles sighed. "Nothing," he said.

"Nothing," Inch repeated.

"Nothing?" said Lily. "You can't do 'nothing'! You're going to be in trouble with Mr. Wooden if you don't do something."

Mr. Wooden walked up behind Lily. "Did I hear my name?" he asked.

Inch and Miles looked up at their teacher.

Lily turned around. She put her hands on her hips. "Inch and Miles say they're doing nothing for International Day. Everybody's doing something. Inch and Miles should too."

Mr. Wooden looked at Inch and Miles and shook his head. "I've never seen such hangdog looks on you two. What's up?"

"We don't want to do a project, Mr. Wooden," said Inch.

"We don't have any good ideas," said Miles.

"What? After all the suggestions I've given you?"

Inch and Miles didn't want to tell their teacher, but none of his ideas had sounded like much fun. Some, to be truthful, sounded boring—like researching a country's crops or government. And they all sounded like way too much work.

Mr. Wooden made a triangle with his fingers.

Inch and Miles knew what Mr. Wooden was getting at. The triangle meant they should think about the Pyramid of Success. Each of the fourteen blocks on the Pyramid helped them be the best they could be.

Whenever Inch and Miles had a problem, one of the blocks on the Pyramid of Success helped them solve it. One time they learned about Hard Work. Another time Cooperation was key. So which block on the Pyramid did they need to remember this time?

Mr. Wooden twirled the silver whistle that hung on a chain around his neck—the magic silver whistle. "Guess you'll probably want to borrow this again?"

Inch and Miles both shrugged.

To be honest, Inch and Miles didn't much care. They had absolutely zip, zero interest in this project. So what if they were the only ones without a project. What did it matter?

"If you don't do something for International Day, boys, what will your parents say . . . and your friends? I hate to say this, but you don't want to look like losers, do you?"

"Losers?" Inch and Miles said. That didn't sound so great. But neither did working on some dumb project. Inch and Miles were, as they say, caught between a rock and a hard place. Maybe the silver whistle was the answer. It had helped them before. Maybe it would this time too.

"OK," said Inch.

"OK," said Miles.

Mr. Wooden smiled and handed the magic silver whistle to Miles. "Good luck, boys. And don't lose this. It can't be replaced!"

CHAPTER 2

Falling into Trouble

Inch and Miles raced out of the classroom, happy to be outdoors in the sunshine. When they reached the edge of the school yard, Inch and Miles huddled together. Miles lifted the magic silver whistle to his lips. But he didn't blow.

"What's the matter?" Inch asked.

Miles sighed. "I don't feel like another adventure right now. Do you?"

"Not really," said Inch.

"Let's just sit here till recess. We'll tell Mr. Wooden the whistle didn't work," said Miles. "And that won't be a lie because it really didn't work."

"Because you didn't blow it," said Inch.

"But we won't mention that," said Miles.

Inch and Miles flopped down on the grass and gazed at the sky. Big puffy clouds floated by. Watching the clouds made Inch and Miles very sleepy. Just as the two friends were about to fall asleep, a loud siren blasted.

Inch jumped up. "What's that?"

"Fire drill!" Miles said. "The whole school will be out in a flash. We've got to get out of here before Mr. Wooden sees us!"

Inch and Miles huddled together, and Miles blew hard on the whistle. The school yard disappeared. Suddenly, Inch and Miles were floating through creamy cotton clouds.

They heard strange sounds like thunder in a bottle, rain in a teakettle, and lightning cracking upside down and sideways. They closed their eyes and plugged their ears. When they opened their eyes, they were sitting on a tree branch in a forest. Below them they heard voices.

"You *can't* leave," someone said.

"We can't do this without you!" said another. "It's not fair!"

When Inch and Miles peered down, they saw Rhonda, the robin they had met on their first magic whistle adventure. Dozens of robins, two squirrels, an opossum, a raccoon, and a wild boar were gathered around her.

A sudden gust of wind shook the tree branch. Inch and Miles tumbled backward. Down they plunged, disappearing headfirst into a pile of leaves. But not before Rhonda and the forest creatures saw them.

Rhonda's eyes opened wide in surprise. "Inch and Miles! What are you doing here?"

"Ah-choo!" Inch sneezed as he crawled out of the leaves.

Miles dusted himself off. "Where are we?" he asked.

At that moment, a parrot wearing a sombrero zipped by and landed on a branch just above them. "Mexico, muchachos. You are in beautiful Mexico. Olé!" squawked the parrot.

"And who are you?" Miles asked the parrot.

"Señor Dude, at your service," he said, tipping his hat and bowing. "But just call me Dude."

Soon all the other forest creatures came ambling toward them with sad and mopey faces. A family of robins flitted over from a nearby tree.

Inch turned toward Rhonda. "And who are all these guys?" Inch asked.

Rhonda stuck out a wing and pointed to the robins. "Well, this is my husband, Rickey, and the rest of my robin family," Rhonda said with a big grin on her beak.

Rickey and the robins darted up into the air, flapping their wings. They made a quick circle and landed on the forest floor.

"And this is my winter family—Sancho, Paco, Rosa, Lola, and Bella . . . and of course Señor Dude."

Inch and Miles couldn't help staring at these animals with their hangdog faces. "What's wrong with them?" Inch asked.

"They look like someone stole their tamales," said Miles.

"We don't want Rhonda to leave," said Señor Dude. "But she has to. She's going to be on *Opral*."

Inch and Miles stared at each other. "*Opral*?" they said.

"You're really going to be on the famous TV show?" Miles asked. "Wow!"

Señor Dude squawked loudly. "Rhonda's become quite famous," the parrot told Inch and Miles.

Rhonda blushed. "You flatter me, Señor Dude," she said.

Rickey flew up to Rhonda and put a wing around her. "Rhonda's the most enthusiastic robin on the planet. Aren't you, Sweetie?"

"Yeah," said Sancho, the opossum. "She's always the first robin to make it back to Cleveland every spring."

A fat raccoon waddled forward. "Opral's going to interview Rhonda at her summer home in Cleveland," Paco told them. "She's bringing her TV crew."

"Opral's going to the tree Rhonda has been nesting in for years," the robins chirped.

"Yeah," said Bella. "Opral's going to ask Rhonda all sorts of questions. You know, the stuff she always asks the guests on her TV show—like 'How do you do it?' and 'Why?' "

Miles scratched his head. "But we heard you guys complaining about Rhonda leaving," Miles said.

"Aren't you happy Rhonda's so famous that she's going to be on TV?" Inch asked.

"NO! Because that means she won't be here to plan the fiesta for the orphans of Santo Miguelo," Sancho grumbled.

"Rhonda always plans the fiesta before she leaves for Cleveland," said Rosa and Lola.

"We can't do it without her!" the whole group wailed.

"What's a fiesta?" Inch and Miles asked.

"A big party!" they exclaimed.

"Well, if planning a party is so hard, don't have one," Inch said.

"We have to! For the orphans!" Sancho, Paco, Rosa, Lola, and Bella said. Señor Dude squawked.

"Listen, everyone," Rhonda said to her friends. "You can make this fiesta happen without me. You just need a couple of good leaders!" She turned to Inch and Miles. A big smile spread across her beak. "Like my friends here!"

Inch and Miles stared at each other. Yikes. What had they gotten themselves into this time? They weren't looking for more work!

CHAPTER 3

More Problems

"Not us!" said Miles. "We don't know anything about fiestas."

"Yeah," said Inch, "nothing."

"Will you please excuse us?" Miles said as he grabbed Inch and dragged him behind the tree.

"I don't want to do this," Miles said to Inch. "Do you?"

"No way," said Inch. "Let's get out of here. Blow the whistle."

 Miles blew
the silver
whistle. Again
they floated
through
creamy
clouds and
heard strange
noises. But when
they opened their
eyes, they stood exactly
where they had been—behind the tree in
the forest.

"Try again!" Inch said.

Miles blew the whistle again with all the
breath he could muster. They floated through
clouds and heard loud noises, but when they
opened their eyes, they saw the same old forest.

Miles groaned. "I think we're stuck here."

Rhonda poked her head behind the tree. "Problems?" she asked.

"Our magic whistle isn't working. We can't get back to school."

"Well, how about lending my friends a hand, then?" Rhonda asked. "I know it's a big favor to ask. But if I don't leave now, I'll never make it to Cleveland in time. My reputation will be ruined."

"Yeah," said Miles. "I guess Opral would be disappointed."

"And her fans," said Inch. "My mom loves that show."

Rhonda put a wing around Inch. "The orphans of Santo Miguelo would be very sad. My winter family would be sad too. They need to have this fiesta. Won't you help them? All it will take is a little Enthusiasm. If you guys help with the fiesta, I'll mention your names on TV. Give you a big 'thanks' right on *Opral*."

"Wow! Wouldn't Mr. Wooden and Room 5 be impressed!" said Inch.

"But we don't have any ideas!" Miles complained.

"Miles is right," said Inch. "We don't even know where to start. My mom plans all my parties."

"Well, just think," said Rhonda, "you can plan whatever you want! And you'll have lots of help—my whole robin family and my winter family—Sancho, Paco, Rosa, Lola, Bella, and Señor Dude."

"But none of them seems to want a party," said Miles.

"Oh, yes they do," Rhonda said. "You just need to light a little fire under them. Get the old ball rolling, as they say."

"And how do we do that?" Inch asked.

"Enthusiasm, fellas, that's how!" Rhonda said, slapping them on the backs. "The energy and pep you show will rub off on those you know. Don't make excuses, complain, or whine. Enjoy your work and success you'll find! Now adios, amigos," Rhonda said. "Gotta fly. Opral awaits!"

CHAPTER 4

Pressure!

From behind the tree, Inch and Miles listened to Rhonda say good-bye to her family and friends. Soon they saw her soar high in the sky on her way to Cleveland and *The Opral Show*.

Miles let out a huge sigh. "Great. What are we going to do now?"

"Be enthusiastic?" Inch asked.

"I don't feel very enthusiastic," said Miles.

"Me either. I feel like I'm going to throw up."

"Well, we can't hide behind this tree much longer," said Miles.

"Hey, dudes. 'Zup?" Señor Dude squawked. He perched on a limb just above them.

Rosa and Lola peeked around the tree trunk.

Paco, Sancho, and Bella slouched up to them with mopey faces.

"So, who's going to be in charge of the fiesta now?" Paco asked Señor Dude.

"These guys," Señor Dude said, nodding toward Inch and Miles.

"They don't look very enthusiastic," Sancho said.

Miles' shoulders sagged. "Amigo," he said, practicing his Spanish, "that's putting it mildly."

"We haven't a clue about fiestas!" Inch said, sighing. "But we promised Rhonda."

"She's going to mention our names on *Opral*," Miles told them.

"Our teacher and the kids at school will be impressed," said Inch.

"Hey, that's totally cool!" Señor Dude said. "Then you guys had better come up with something good."

The forest creatures stared at Inch and Miles, waiting.

This was too much pressure. Inch started to shake. How were they going to pull off a party with this droopy group?

Miles poked Inch. "OK, Inch," he whispered. "Shape up. Smile! Act enthusiastic! Do it for Rhonda and the orphans."

Inch stretched up as tall as he could. He plastered a smile on his face. "So hey, everybody," Inch said. "If we're going to have a fiesta, what do you say we make it the best ever?"

Miles jumped up and snapped his arms out like a cheerleader.

The creatures said nothing. They crouched on the forest floor like a bunch of dead fleas on a mule.

Inch climbed onto a fallen log and stared down at Rhonda's friends. It felt great looking down at them instead of up. He grinned wide. "Hey, dudes! Let's get some ideas going here," Inch said. "So what do you do at a fiesta?" he asked, stretching as tall as he could.

Rickey flew onto the log beside Inch. The robin family followed.

"Ah . . . play games," Paco said.

"We always have a piñata," Sancho said.

"Dance," said Rosa and Lola. "The Mexican hat dance." The squirrel sisters gave a little demonstration.

"Eat," Bella said. "Tacos, burritos, and lots of salsa!"

"Now there's an idea you can sink your tusks into!" Miles said with a giggle. He felt a little tingle of excitement. He loved tacos—with lots of cheese, of course.

"Don't forget the music," Señor Dude said. "We always have a mariachi band."

"Cool," said Inch. "What about decorations?" he asked.

"Yeah," said Rosa. "The decorations *are* cool. The robins hang chili pepper lights on the tree branches. We make tissue paper cutouts, glue them on a string, and hang them everywhere."

"She means *papel picado*," Señor Dude told Inch and Miles. "Tissue paper cutouts. Very popular in Mexico."

"We love making papel picado," Rosa and Lola said.

"We love to hang them," said the robins.

"Now that's the enthusiasm we need!" Miles said. "Right, Inch?"

"Ah . . . I guess so . . . but . . . " Inch stared at something he saw lurking at the forest's edge. "I think we might be in big trouble."

All the creatures turned around to take a look.

It was a wolf. And he was staring at Bella, drool dripping from his huge, open mouth.

Sancho fell over and played dead.

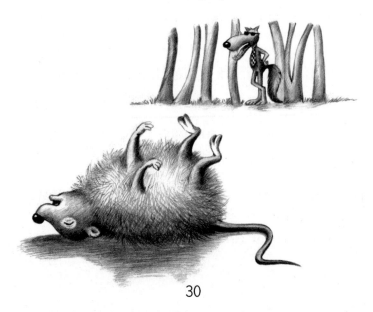

CHAPTER 5

What Now?

At the sight of the wolf, Miles lost his enthusiasm.

Inch started shaking.

"Yo, Lupe!" Señor Dude called to the wolf. "Come join the party!"

Rosa and Lola poked Sancho. "Get up. It's only Lupe."

Sancho opened his eyes. He shut them again when Lupe loped toward him, his mouth hanging open.

"Amigos!" the wolf said. "What's up?" He smiled wide at Bella.

"Didn't you hear?" Señor Dude said. "Rhonda's going to be on *The Opral Show*," he told Lupe. "She's taken off early for Cleveland. She left these dudes in charge of the fiesta." He nodded toward Inch and Miles.

Inch smiled at Lupe, even though he felt like running away.

Miles smiled, too, even though he felt like playing dead like Sancho.

This Lupe guy had a huge mouth with huge teeth. Lupe opened his mouth wide and said, *"Bueno"* (which means "good" in Spanish). "How can I help?"

Inch wanted to say, "You can help by leaving."

Miles wanted to say, "You can help by wiping the drool off your mouth." But instead he said, "What can you do?"

"Anything you want," said Lupe. "I am what you call 'multitalented.'" He grinned at Bella, his tongue lolling and dripping with drool.

Bella sidestepped around Sancho, who was still playing dead. She stood close to Rosa and Lola.

"OK," said Miles. "Let's see what we have so far. Inch?" He poked Inch, who couldn't take his eyes off Lupe's teeth.

"Oh, yeah, ah . . . the fiesta," Inch tried to say with pep in his voice. "Um . . . for the fiesta we need decorations, food, and music. Who will do the decorations?"

Silence.

"How about the food?"

Silence.

"Music?" This time Inch tried to show some pep and energy by doing a little dance.

Lupe opened his mouth wide. "Ay, ay, ay, ay!" he sang loudly. *"Canta y no llores"* (which means "sing and don't cry" in Spanish).

Señor Dude landed on Lupe's head and began singing too. "Ay, ay, ay, ay!"

Soon all Rhonda's friends, even Sancho, joined in the song, while the robins chirped and danced in the sky.

Inch and Miles sang and danced, too, until they were both out of breath.

Finally Miles shouted, "All *right*! How 'bout we use a little bit of this enthusiasm to get the fiesta planned? Paco, you're in charge of games. Rosa and Lola, entertainment. Bella, you'll do food. Sancho, Señor Dude, and all the robins will help with decorations. Lupe, you're our music man."

"I'll round up my band!" said Lupe.

"Hooray!" Rosa and Lola shouted. "Mariachi music!"

"And food!" said Bella.

"Tacos, burritos, and enchiladas!" said Paco. "And lots of salsa."

"And cheese!" said Miles. His mouth was watering already.

"Who will help Bella with the food?" Inch asked.

"I will," Sancho said.

"Super!" said Inch.

"We'll hang the papel picado and the chili pepper lights," said Rickey.

"Now you're talking!" said Miles.

"You're all so enthusiastic," said Inch. He was beginning to feel that way too.

"Wait a minute," said Señor Dude. "I think we may have a problem." He pointed to a calendar tacked on a tree trunk.

Everyone stared at the calendar. One day had a big red circle around it. In all the excitement about the fiesta, everyone had forgotten about this important day. And it was tomorrow.

"Oh, no!" everyone groaned.

"What's the matter?" asked Inch.

"We're in big trouble," said Paco.

Sancho fell over and played dead.

Uh-oh, thought Inch and Miles. What now?

CHAPTER 6

Leaving for Cleveland

"What's the matter?" Inch asked.

"The robins," Señor Dude said. "They have to leave for Cleveland . . . tomorrow!"

The robins had gotten so caught up in the excitement of the fiesta plans, they had forgotten they had to leave.

"Can't you wait a few days?" asked Miles.

"We have to leave. The news about Rhonda has leaked out. So all the robins are fleeing their winter homes even earlier this year. We don't want to lose out on all the best nesting places," Rickey told Miles.

Inch and Miles watched Paco, Rosa, Lola, Bella, Lupe, and even Señor Dude go all sad and droopy again. Sancho was still playing dead. Inch and Miles knew they had to do something.

"I know!" said Miles. "How about hanging the papel picado now?"

"Great idea!" said Inch. "That shouldn't take too long, should it?"

"No," said Rosa. "But we haven't even made them yet!"

Everyone sighed.

"This fiesta is going to be a flop without strings of papel picado," Rosa and Lola said.

"Well then," said Inch with all the enthusiasm he could muster, "what about the chili pepper lights? Can you hang those?"

"Yeah," everyone said. "Hang the chili pepper lights. Please?"

All at once, the robins took off, soaring high above the forest floor.

"Where are they going?" Inch asked, as he watched the robins disappear.

"Cleveland!" the forest friends shouted.

"There goes our fiesta," said Paco. "The robins always hang the strings of papel picado and the chili pepper lights. No one else can do it."

"What's a fiesta without chili pepper lights?" asked Rosa.

"Nothing, that's what," moaned Lola.

"Well, we can still have music, food, and dancing!" Miles offered.

"That sounds like fun," said Inch.

"Not enough," said Paco.

"Our fiesta would be a dud without decorations," said Rosa.

"A flop," agreed Bella.

"A bore," said Lupe, smiling at Bella.

Sancho said nothing. He was still playing dead.

Inch and Miles looked at each other. They had to do something. Rhonda and the orphans were depending on them. They had to have the fiesta.

"Look!" said Miles, pointing toward the sky.

"The robins!" Inch said. "They're coming back!"

The robins skidded to a landing on the forest floor. "We've talked it over," Rickey said. "We've got to do this for Rhonda . . . and the orphans. We'll stay long enough to hang the decorations."

"Hooray!" everyone shouted.

"Olé!" squawked Señor Dude.

"Fiesta!" cheered Inch and Miles.

Rosa poked Sancho. "Wake up! We're going to make the papel picado!"

"That's the spirit!" said Miles. "Let's get started. Rosa and Lola, what do we need for the papel picado?"

"Tissue paper and scissors," said Rosa.

"Glue and string," said Lola.

"And where do we get those?" Inch asked.

"In the fiesta chest," Paco said. "Where we keep all our fiesta supplies."

"We'll go get the chest," Sancho said. "Come on, Paco. *Vamonos*" (which means "let's go" in Spanish)!

Lupe smiled at Bella. "I'll help too," he said. He loped over to Paco and Sancho.

"That's the enthusiasm we need!" Miles said.

"This is going to be the best fiesta ever!" Inch said. "Rhonda will be proud!"

"Opral will be impressed!" Miles said.

"The orphans will be happy!" squawked Señor Dude.

"We'll all have fun!" everyone shouted.

Paco, Sancho, and Lupe ran off to get the fiesta chest. When they returned, everyone gathered around the brightly painted chest. Rickey and the robins perched on top.

"OK, folks," Miles said. "Open it up, and let's get going!"

Paco tried opening the chest. "It's locked," he said.

"Who has the key?" Inch asked.

Everyone looked at one another.

"Uh-oh," said Rickey. "Rhonda does!"

"Oh, no," whined Paco. "What are we going to do now?"

CHAPTER 7

Doomed?

"Doesn't anyone know where Rhonda keeps the key?" Miles asked.

Rickey shook his head. "Sorry, guys."

Inch and Miles had to do something before everyone gave up again.

"I know," said Miles. "If we all search for the key, I'm sure we'll find it!" He spoke with as much enthusiasm as he could muster.

"Forget it, amigo," Lupe said. "Have you noticed how big this forest is? We could look for days, even weeks, and never find that key."

All the forest creatures hung their heads. "We're doomed," Lola moaned.

Sancho started to play dead.

Señor Dude squawked and poked Sancho with his beak. "Hold on, amigo. We're not doomed yet. I think I can help."

"You can?" said Inch.

"*Sí*" (which means "yes" in Spanish), Señor Dude squawked. "In a former life I learned a skill that I'm not too proud of . . . but it may come in handy here."

Sad, droopy eyes turned curious as they focused on Señor Dude.

"What is it, Dude?" Lupe asked.

"Picking locks," Señor Dude confessed

After Señor Dude picked the lock, everyone set to work on the decorations (although it was really more like fun than work!). The robins began hanging the chili pepper lights on the trees. Inch and Miles and Rhonda's winter friends snipped and snapped tissue paper into papel picado. Everyone sang as they cut and pasted and strung and hung. It felt almost like a fiesta already. Soon they had strings and strings of papel picado. Whenever one string was finished, the robins hung it around the clearing where the fiesta would take place.

"This is going to be so awesome!" Inch said, gazing at the strings of papel picado and the red chili pepper lights.

"Awesome is right!" said Miles.

"Si, si, si!!!" The forest friends shouted. "Fiesta grande!"

When the last string of papel picado and chili pepper lights had been hung, the robins said good-bye. "Adios, amigos," they called as they flew off toward their summer homes in Cleveland. "See you next winter. Have a wonderful fiesta!"

Inch and Miles looked around the forest clearing. Strings of papel picado fluttered in the breeze. Chili pepper lights twinkled in the tree branches. Everything looked so festive.

"Wow!" said Inch.

"Amazing!" said Miles. He felt a tingle of excitement imagining fiesta day—the music, the games, the fun, and the food. He imagined seeing the happy faces of the orphans and hearing their squeals of delight. Already he could taste the crunchy tacos . . . with lots of cheese!

For the next several days, the forest creatures were very, very busy. They planned games. They shopped. They hung the piñata. They prepared food. While Señor Dude, Sancho, Paco, Bella, Rosa, and Lola worked getting everything ready for the big day, Lupe practiced with his mariachi band.

Everyone sang as they worked. "Ay, ay, ay, ay. Let's have a party. A fiesta *muy grande*. Ay, ay, ay, ay."

Inch and Miles pitched in whenever someone needed help.

"You guys are fantastic!" Miles said often.

"You really know how to throw a party!" Inch kept repeating.

But not everything always went smoothly. Bella burned a big batch of taco meat. Señor Dude flew into a string of chili pepper lights. Rosa and Lola accidentally smashed the hat for the Mexican hat dance. Lupe drooled in the salsa.

When something went wrong, Inch or Miles would say. "That's OK. It can be fixed. *No problemo*" (which means "no problem" in Spanish). They were determined not to let their new friends lose heart. This was going to be the best fiesta ever. Fiesta grande—muy grande! The best fiesta in the whole wide world!

Finally, the day before the fiesta, everything was ready.

"You did it, friends!" Miles said. "This fiesta is going to be so awesome. Now go to bed and get a good rest. Tomorrow's the big day."

But Inch and Miles were still worried. Would everything go as planned?

CHAPTER 8

Fiesta! Olé!

The next morning everyone woke up bright and early. They all gathered in the forest clearing. Their leaders, Inch and Miles, stood above them on the fallen log.

"I'm nervous," said Paco.

"I wonder if Rhonda made it," said Rosa and Lola.

"I'm sure she did," Miles said. "She'll be on *Opral* today."

"I feel sick," said Bella.

"I'm not ready for this," said Lupe.

"I can't do this," said Sancho.

"What if it rains?" squawked Señor Dude.

All the forest creatures grumbled, moaned, and whined. Inch and Miles could see a disaster brewing. What were they going to do?

They had to think of something . . . and quick!

"What would Rhonda do?" That is the thought that flickered through Inch and Miles' minds. Immediately, both friends had the same answer—show Enthusiasm!

"You guys can do it!" Inch and Miles said in one voice.

"I've never seen such cooperation and hard work," said Inch.

"You were awesome," said Miles.

"Amazing," said Inch.

That's when Inch and Miles heard loud rumbling sounds. It couldn't be thunder . . . and rain . . . could it? They had their answer soon enough.

"Look!" Señor Dude squawked.

A pair of trucks bounced into the clearing. They were loaded with all sorts of equipment— lights, miles of electrical cord, video cameras, and TV monitors.

A bearded man wearing a baseball cap jumped out of the first truck. "So where's the fiesta?" he asked.

"Here!" the surprised group said.

"We're televising," the man said. "Your fiesta is going to be on *The Opral Show.*"

"What?" cried Rosa and Lola.

"I can't believe it!" said Sancho and Paco.

"We're celebrities," squawked Señor Dude.

"Oh, my gosh!" Bella said. "How do I look?"

Lupe smiled and drooled. "Beautiful!" he said.

"All right," Miles said. "Places everyone!"

While the camera crew set up its equipment, Inch and Miles and all the forest creatures readied everything for the fiesta.

Soon the orphans arrived, along with a steady stream of folks from the village of Santo Miguelo. As they made their way to the forest clearing, Lupe and his mariachi band greeted them with music. The aroma of tacos, enchiladas, and burritos wafted through the air. Chili pepper lights twinkled from the tree branches. Strings of papel picado fluttered in the breeze. On a small stage, Rosa and Lola did the Mexican hat dance.

"Tacos, enchiladas, and burritos!" Bella shouted.

Sancho and Paco stood underneath the donkey piñata they had hung on a tree branch.

"Come, everyone. Time for the piñata!" Sancho shouted.

Paco blindfolded the little kids, who took turns hitting the papier-mâché donkey with a stick.

During all the excitement, no one noticed that the TV cameras had been filming or that a TV monitor had been set up. The fiesta was being broadcast to TV stations all across Mexico and the United States.

"Time for *Opral*!" one of the TV crewmen announced.

"Rhonda!" All of the fiesta-goers shouted as they ran to gather around the TV.

To their surprise, they saw themselves—and their fiesta! Then the fiesta scene faded and Opral appeared.

"We're here today in Cleveland," Opral said. "My special guest is Rhonda Robin." The camera panned in to a close-up of Rhonda, who smiled brightly.

"Congratulations, Rhonda," Opral said. "You did it again. You're the very first robin to return to Cleveland. To what do you owe your success?"

Rhonda blushed a bright pink. "Well," she said, smiling at the camera, "my winter family in Mexico can tell you. And so can my new friends, Inch and Miles, who helped put on that wonderful fiesta you just saw."

One of the cameras zoomed in on Inch and Miles. They looked at the TV monitor and saw themselves. They heard Opral's voice ask, "So, Inch and Miles, what is it that makes Rhonda able to create such a fine home for herself in Cleveland and you to put on such a fabulous fiesta there in the forest?"

"Well …" Inch stuttered, then smiled at the camera. "Hi, Mom. I'll be home pretty soon." Miles poked Inch. "Ah, ah . . . a lot of things . . . ah . . . "

"See these guys?" Miles pointed to Paco, Sancho, Rosa, Lola, Bella, Lupe, and Señor Dude. "They all worked really hard and cooperated."

"But—" said Inch. He stared into the camera and smiled. "Hi, Mr. Wooden! Hi, Lily and Room 5!" Miles poked Inch again. "The main thing we found out was—" Inch said. "We needed to have . . ." he glanced at Miles.

"Enthusiasm!" they both shouted.

"Well," said Opral. "From the looks of things there, I'd say your Enthusiasm worked. Your fiesta for the orphans of Santo Miguelo appears to have been a great success."

"Thanks, Opral," said Inch.

"Thanks, Rhonda," said Miles.

"Oh!" said Inch. "Mr. Wooden and Lily, if you're watching, we have our project for International Day—a fiesta."

"A fiesta muy grande!" said Miles.

"Olé!" squawked Señor Dude.

EPILOGUE

After the fiesta, Inch and Miles said good-bye to their new friends. Miles blew the silver whistle. This time the magic worked. Soon Inch and Miles were back in Room 5 with Mr. Wooden and the rest of the class. Of course, everyone thought they were big stars for being on *The Opral Show* and all. Everyone was very excited, too, about the fiesta that Inch and Miles were planning for International Day. Inch and Miles were excited also. They had all the good ideas they needed. Now all it would take is hard work, cooperation, and a lot of Enthusiasm! Olé!

ABOUT THE AUTHORS

Coach and teacher **John Wooden** is a towering figure in 20th-century American sports. His UCLA basketball teams virtually created "March Madness" by amassing 10 national championships, 7 in a row; along with 4 perfect seasons; an 88-game winning streak; and 38 straight victories in tournament play.

Sports Illustrated says, "There has never been a finer man in American sports, or a finer coach."

Coach Wooden has two children, seven grandchildren, and eleven great-grandchildren.
(Visit CoachJohnWooden.com)

Steve Jamison is a best-selling author, award-winning television producer, and public speaker.
(Visit SteveJamison.com)

Bonnie Graves is the author of 13 books for young readers, both fiction and nonfiction. Beginning with *The Best Worst Day* in 1996, she has received several awards and honors for her work, including a 2005 South Carolina Children's Book Award nomination for her chapter book *Taking Care of Trouble.*